Where Once
There Was a Wood

For Indigo, Sam, Emily,
Molly, and Rachel—The Future

Henry Holt and Company, LLC
Publishers since 1866
115 West 18th Street
New York, New York 10011

Henry Holt is a registered trademark
of Henry Holt and Company, LLC.

Library of Congress Cataloging-in-Publication Data
Fleming, Denise.
    Where Once There Was a Wood / Denise Fleming
    Includes bibliographical references.
    Summary: Examines the many forms of wildlife that can be displaced
if their environment is destroyed by development and discusses how
communities and schools can provide spaces for them to live.
    1. Wildlife attracting—Juvenile literature.   2. Wildlife
conservation—Juvenile literature.   [1. Wildlife attracting.
2. Wildlife conservation.]   I. Title.
QL59.F58   1996   639.9—dc20   95-18906

ISBN 0-8050-3761-6 (hardcover)
15 14 13 12 11 10 9 8 7 6 5 4
ISBN 0-8050-6482-6 (paperback)
15 14 13 12 11 10 9 8 7 6 5

First published in hardcover in 1996 by Henry Holt and Company
First Owlet paperback edition—2000
Printed in the United States of America on acid-free paper. ∞

Book design by Denise Fleming and David Powers.
The artist used cotton rag fiber to create the illustrations for this book.

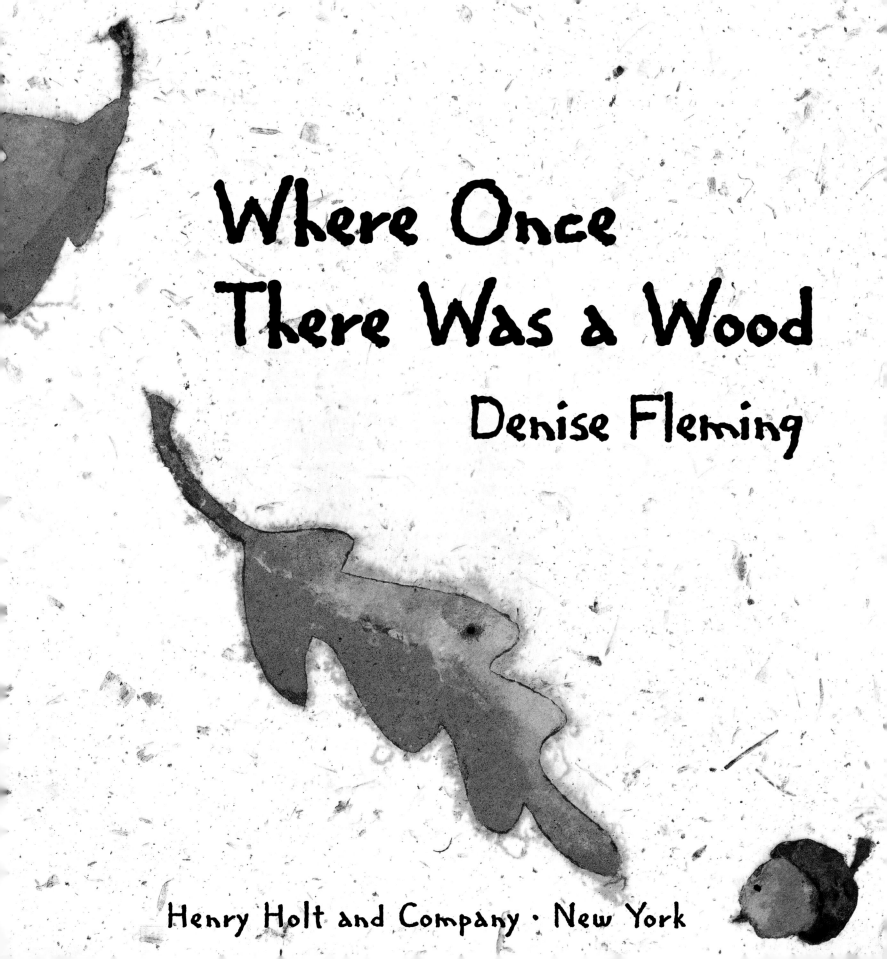

Where Once There Was a Wood

Denise Fleming

Henry Holt and Company · New York

Where once
there was a wood

a meadow

and a creek

where once
the red fox rested
and closed his eyes
to sleep

where once
the ferns unfurled
and purple violets grew

where once
the woodchuck left his den
to catch the morning dew

where once
the horned owl hunted
to feed her hungry brood

where once the heron fished
and sp ar ' his glitt ring fond

where once the brown snake
slithered and slipped out of sight

where once the raccoons rambled
and rummaged in the night

where once the berries ripened
and waxwings came to feed

where once
the pheasants roosted
and f d n r ts and d

Where once there was a wood

a road-ward walk!

sit houses side by side

twenty houses deep.

Welcome Wildlife

Wild areas are disappearing. Housing developments and shopping malls are taking over land that once was home to wildlife. We can provide new homes for wild creatures by creating wildlife habitats in our backyards, school yards, and community spaces.

to your
Backyard Habitat

(Habitat: The place where a plant or animal naturally lives and grows.)

When planning your backyard habitat, consider the climate, location, and soil of the area. Keep in mind the needs of local wildlife and the needs of wild creatures that stop over during migration. Study your space. Pretend you're a bird, butterfly, or animal. Are there places to hide? What about food? Are there fruit- and seed-bearing plants? Wildflowers? Is there water? Make a list of what your space provides and what is needed. Research native plants. Visit a nature center. Talk to local naturalists. They will be able to answer many of your questions about native plants and wildlife.

Wild creatures have four basic needs:
space, shelter, water, and food.

Space ━━━━━━

Wild creatures need space to live and raise their young. Backyards, school yards, and community areas can provide this space.

Shelter

Shelter provides places for wildlife to roost, nest, hide, and be safe from harsh weather. Trees, bushes, and ground-hugging plants all provide shelter for wildlife. Needled evergreens keep birds and animals snug during cold winters. Dense thickets and brambles such as raspberries and blackberries offer excellent hiding places, nesting sites, and a bounty of berries in summer. Variety is important when planting for shelter. Create open areas and closed areas. Mix tall trees and low shrubs. Choose plants that provide shelter *and* food.

A yard that is too tidy is not attractive to wildlife. Grass clippings, small branches, leaves, and moss can be used by wildlife as nesting material. Lower branches should be left on shrubs to provide cover for animals. Rock piles and stone walls shelter small creatures such as chipmunks, lizards, and toads. Brush piles offer places for rabbits and birds to rest, nest, and hide.

Build a brush pile by heaping brush and branches over logs. A discarded Christmas tree is an excellent base to pile brush and branches over. It's important that there be inside spaces where birds can perch and small animals can hide. During summer months flowering vines such as scarlet runner beans or morning glories can be grown over the brush pile.

Birdhouses, bat houses, squirrel houses, and nesting shelves can be built to provide additional shelter for wildlife.

- Do not use herbicides, fungicides, or insecticides.
- After brushing your dog or cat, place loose fur outdoors for birds to use as nesting material.
- Provide a small patch of mud for robins and swallows to use when building their nests.

Water

Wild creatures need water for drinking and bathing. A large clay plant saucer filled with water and placed on the ground will attract small animals. An elevated birdbath provides water for birds and protects them from cats. Fresh clean water should always be available. During cold months a birdbath heater may be needed to keep water from freezing.

A backyard pond provides a home for fish, turtles, and frogs, and a place for toads and dragonflies to lay their eggs. Different water depths should be created in the pond, particularly shallow areas for drinking and bathing. Water plants provide shelter and food. Water lilies shade fish, roots of floating plants support fish eggs, and cattails and sedges provide shelter and nesting material.

Purple Coneflower

Food

Food for wildlife is best provided by growing plants. Nuts, grasses, berries, seeds, buds, nectar, and pollen are all food for wildlife. Select a variety of plants that provide food year-round. Blackberries provide food in summer, dogwood berries provide food in fall, while winterberries stay on the bush until late winter. Nuts and seeds can be stored by chipmunks, mice, and squirrels to be eaten when food is scarce.

Fruits and berries are relished by birds, opossums, and raccoons. Plant a fruit salad hedgerow—a thicket of small fruit trees, berry bushes, and fruiting vines. A place for wildlife to feast, nest, and hide.

Allow an area of grass to grow wild and produce seed, providing both food and protective cover for rabbits and birds. Wildflowers such as coneflowers, goldenrod, and sunflowers provide color in the garden, pollen and nectar for bees and butterflies, and seeds for birds and small animals. Bees are important to the backyard habitat. Their presence insures pollination, which means more berries and seeds for wildlife.

Feeding stations may be set up to supplement natural food sources. Sunflower seeds, millet, cracked corn, and suet are popular with wild creatures.

Trees and shrubs that provide food and shelter

Birch	Currant	Honeysuckle	Oak
Blackberry	Dogwood	Huckleberry	Pine
Blueberry	Elderberry	Juniper	Raspberry
Cherry	Fir	Mountain ash	Serviceberry
Crabapple	Hawthorn	Mulberry	Winterberry

Butterfly and hummingbird garden

A sunny spot planted with nectar-rich flowers will attract butterflies and hummingbirds. Hummingbirds are especially drawn to red flowers.

- A hummingbird feeder filled with sugar water will lure hummingbirds to the garden.
- Moths may visit the butterfly garden at night in search of nectar.
- Butterflies sun to raise their body temperature and warm their muscles for flight.

Flowers that attract butterflies and hummingbirds

Bee balm	Coreopsis	Honeysuckle	Mexican sunflower	Salvia
Black-eyed Susan	Cosmos	Jewelweed	Milkweed	Sunflower
Butterfly bush	Daylily	Joe-pye weed	Nicotiana	Thistle
Butterfly weed	Foxglove	Lantana	Petunia	Trumpet vine
Cardinal flower	Gayfeather	Lavender	Phlox	Yarrow
Columbine	Goldenrod	Marigold	Purple coneflower	Zinnia

Planting bushes or flowers that are attractive to a particular creature does not guarantee a visit from that creature.

More information

The National Wildlife Federation has established the Backyard Wildlife Habitat Program to encourage people to create wildlife habitats across the United States. For information about the program, write: National Wildlife Federation, Backyard Wildlife Habitat Program, 1400 16th St. N.W., Washington, DC 20036-2266.

Allison, James
Water in the Garden
Boston: Little Brown and Company, 1991

Dennis, James V.
The Wildlife Gardener
New York: Alfred A. Knopf, 1985

Druse, Ken
The Natural Habitat Garden
New York: Clarkson Potter Publishers, 1994

Editors of Sunset Books
and Sunset Magazine
An Illustrated Guide to Attracting Birds
Menlo Park, CA: Sunset Publishing Corporation, 1990

Harrison, Kit and George
America's Favorite Backyard Wildlife
New York: Simon & Schuster, 1985

McKinley, Michael
How to Attract Birds
San Francisco: Ortho Books, 1983

Meriless, Bill
Attracting Backyard Wildlife
Stillwater, MN: Voyageur Press, 1989

Stein, Sara
Noah's Garden
New York: Houghton Mifflin Company, 1993

Tufts, Craig
The Backyard Naturalist
Washington, DC: National Wildlife Federation, 1988

Xertes Society, in association with
the Smithsonian Institution
Butterfly Gardening
San Francisco: Sierra Club Books, 1990

I also find the Audubon Society Field Guide series very helpful for identifying wildlife and plants.